handsome me

written by wanda thomas
illustrated by john higgins

To my family, Tony, my godsons, David
and Jordan, and the children of
Harlem--to whom
I owe my inspiration.
--W.T.

To my loving wife and family.
--J.H..

It was a bright, sunny day. Everyone was in the playground. As Trevor walked by, his friends yelled out to him.

"Hey, Trevor!" Eric shouted. He stood on the basketball court where several boys were already playing.

"Hey, Eric!" Trevor shouted back through the fence. "What's up?"

"Come shoot some hoops with us," Eric said.

"Sure," Trevor said, then ran through the opening in the playground's wire fence.

His foot barely touched the court when the ball came sailing out of the air toward him. In one smooth move, he caught the ball, ran up to the basket and made a perfect shot off of the backboard.

As they played, a small group of girls gathered at the court to watch. It was hard not to notice Trevor. He had skills way beyond those of the other players, and the girls immediately began talking about him.

"That boy can play some basketball," said a girl named Joy.

"Oh, look! He's coming this way," said another girl named Tanya, as Trevor moved down the court again to make a fast play.

Even though he was playing, Trevor had noticed the girls. So, he smiled and began a series of cool moves to impress them.

He dribbled the ball fast, then slow. He pushed it through his legs, then around his back before shooting it perfectly into the hoop.

"Nothing but net," he beamed.

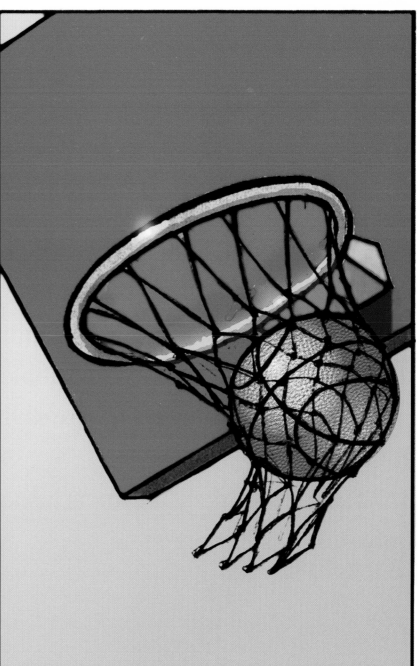

"I think he's soooo cute," Tanya said. "I love to watch him play ball. He sure can dribble."

"Uh-uh," said Ashley, a third girl in the group. "He is ugly. Look at him."

"No he is not," said Tanya. "He is too cute!"

At that moment Trevor was approaching them again. As he stopped to dribble, he could hear everything they were saying about him.

The girls studied Trevor as he began to move down the court again.

"See! Really look at his face. He is ugly," Ashley said softly, but not soft enough to keep Trevor from hearing her.

"He's nothing but skin and bones," Ashley continued.

"You're right. He is ugly," Tanya said. Joy nodded in agreement.

"You're only saying he's cute because he can play basketball," Ashley said.

Trevor couldn't believe his ears. He pretended to be unaffected and ran up and made another perfect shot.

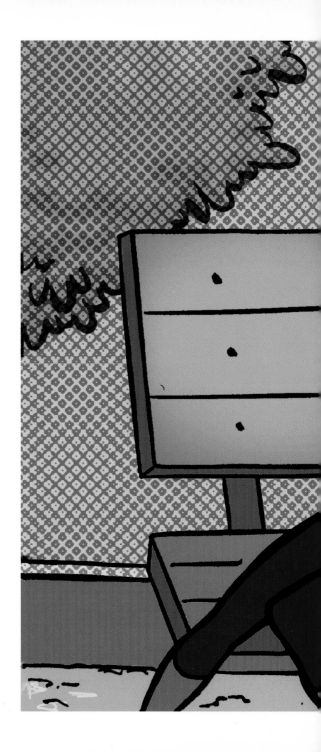

As he walked home from the game, Trevor tried not to think about the things the girls had said. He told himself that everything was cool, that he didn't care what those girls said about him. But deep, down inside, his feelings were really hurt.

T revor had always considered himself a good looking guy, and, definitely, a cool one. In his bedroom, he looked in the mirror that hung from his closet door.

"I have nice smooth, brown skin," he said. "My eyebrows are thick and dark."

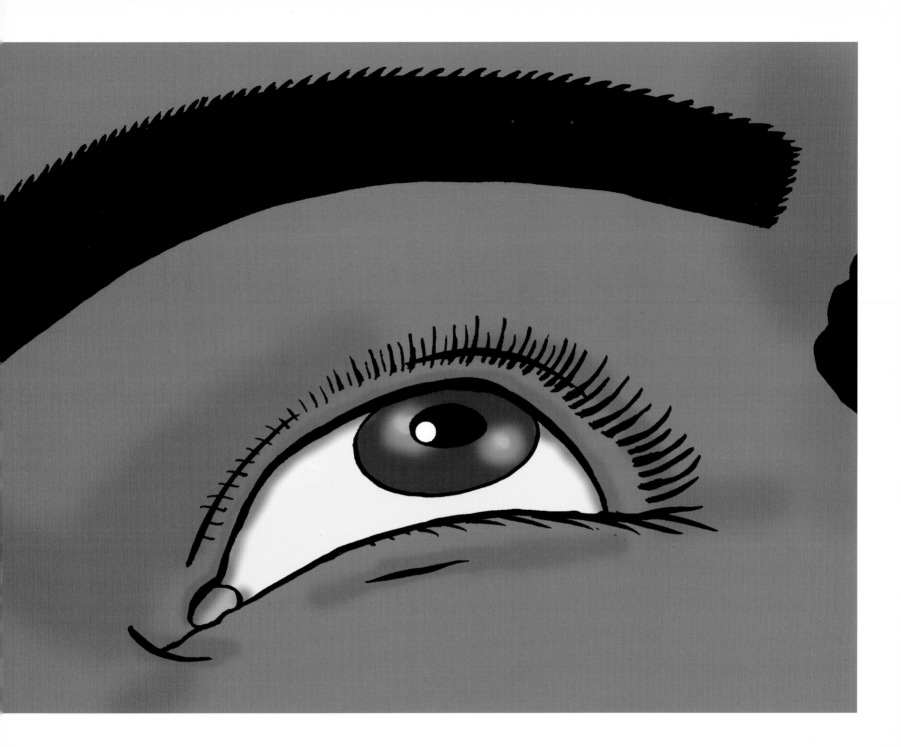

"I have a nice strong jaw. And as soon as I start to work out," he said flexing his biceps, "I'll have large muscles that all the girls will love—including Ashley."

"When I get older, I'll have a smooth mustache and probably some sideburns just like Dad's."

"And look at my clothes," he said. "I'm always clean and neat."

After a careful and critical examination of himself, Trevor felt very proud and satisfied.

He smiled at his reflection in the mirror and said:

"Well, I don't know what those girls were talking about, because all I see is one handsome, cool dude. Me!"

JCW Enterprises Order Form

	Quantity	Code	Price
Book			
Beautiful Me	_____	B001	$8.99
Handsome Me	_____	H001	$8.99
Bookmarks			
Beautiful Me	_____	BB001	$2.00
Handsome Me	_____	HB001	$2.00
Poster			
Beautiful Me / Handsome Me	_____	HP001	$5.00

Send to:

First Name:_____Last Name:_____

*This is a gift from: _____

Street Address:_____Apt. #:_____

City: _____State:_____Zip/PostalCode:_____

(If outside of the U.S.) Province:_____ Country:_____

Email Address:_____PhoneNumber: _____

Billing Address (*If different*):

First Name:_____Last Name:_____

Street Address:_____Apt. #:_____

City: _____State:_____Zip/PostalCode:_____

(If outside of the U.S.) Province:_____ Country:_____

Email Address:_____PhoneNumber: _____

Please make checks payable to **JCW Enterprises**
Send order forms and checks to: **JCW Enterprises, P.O. Box 361, New York, NY 10035**
Tel. No.: 1-800-942-8623

For more items, or to order on-line, go to: *www.wandathomasbooks.com*

PLEASE FEEL FREE TO PHOTOCOPY ORDER FORM

JCW Enterprises Order Form

	Quantity	Code	Price
Book			
Beautiful Me	_____	B001	$8.99
Handsome Me	_____	H001	$8.99
Bookmarks			
Beautiful Me	_____	BB001	$2.00
Handsome Me	_____	HB001	$2.00
Poster			
Beautiful Me / Handsome Me	_____	HP001	$5.00

Send to:

First Name:_____ Last Name:_____

*This is a gift from: _____

Street Address:_____ Apt. #:_____

City: _____ State:_____ Zip/PostalCode:_____

*(If outside of the U.S.) Province:*_____ *Country*:_____

Email Address:_____ PhoneNumber: _____

Billing Address (*If different*):

First Name:_____ Last Name:_____

Street Address:_____ Apt. #:_____

City: _____ State:_____ Zip/PostalCode:_____

*(If outside of the U.S.) Province:*_____ *Country*:_____

Email Address:_____ PhoneNumber: _____

Please make checks payable to **JCW Enterprises**
Send order forms and checks to: **JCW Enterprises, P.O. Box 361, New York, NY 10035**
Tel. No.: 1-800-942-8623

For more items, or to order on-line, go to: _www.wandathomasbooks.com_

PLEASE FEEL FREE TO PHOTOCOPY ORDER FORM

JCW Enterprises Order Form

	Quantity	Code	Price
Book			
Beautiful Me	_____	B001	$8.99
Handsome Me	_____	H001	$8.99
Bookmarks			
Beautiful Me	_____	BB001	$2.00
Handsome Me	_____	HB001	$2.00
Poster			
Beautiful Me / Handsome Me	_____	HP001	$5.00

Send to:

First Name:_____Last Name:_____

*This is a gift from: _____

Street Address:_____Apt. #:_____

City: _____State:_____Zip/PostalCode:_____

*(If outside of the U.S.) Province:*_____ *Country*:_____

Email Address:_____PhoneNumber: _____

Billing Address (*If different*):

First Name:_____Last Name:_____

Street Address:_____Apt. #:_____

City: _____State:_____Zip/PostalCode:_____

*(If outside of the U.S.) Province:*_____ *Country*:_____

Email Address:_____PhoneNumber: _____

Please make checks payable to **JCW Enterprises**
Send order forms and checks to: **JCW Enterprises, P.O. Box 361, New York, NY 10035**
Tel. No.: 1-800-942-8623

For more items, or to order on-line, go to: *www.wandathomasbooks.com*

PLEASE FEEL FREE TO PHOTOCOPY ORDER FORM